JAN BRETT

ON NOAH'S ARK

G. P. PUTNAM'S SONS
NEW YORK

For Gavin Li Ang Hearne

Thanks to our guides, Ali Tiego and Abel Guly

Published simultaneously in Canada. Manufactured
in China by South China Printing Co. Ltd.
Designed by Gunta Alexander. Text set in Breughel.
The art was done in watercolors and gouache.
Airbrush backgrounds by Joseph Hearne.
Library of Congress Cataloging-in-Publication Data
Brett, Jan, 1949– On Noah's ark / Jan Brett. p. cm.
Summary: Noah's granddaughter helps him bring the
animals onto the ark, calm them down, and get them
to sleep. 1. Noah (Biblical figure)—Juvenile fiction.
[1. Noah (Biblical figure)—Fiction. 2. Noah's ark—Fiction.
3. Animals—Fiction. 4. Grandfathers—Fiction.] I. Title.
PZ7.B7559On 2003   [E]—dc21   2003001281
ISBN 0-399-24028-4
1 3 5 7 9 10 8 6 4 2
First Impression

Grandpa Noah says
that the rains are coming.
Soon the land will be
covered with water.

Grandpa Noah is building
an ark for our family
and the animals to live on
until it stops raining.

The ark is ready.

The animals
go in
two by two.

Big animals thump
and bump onto the ark.

Middle-sized animals
clip-clop by.

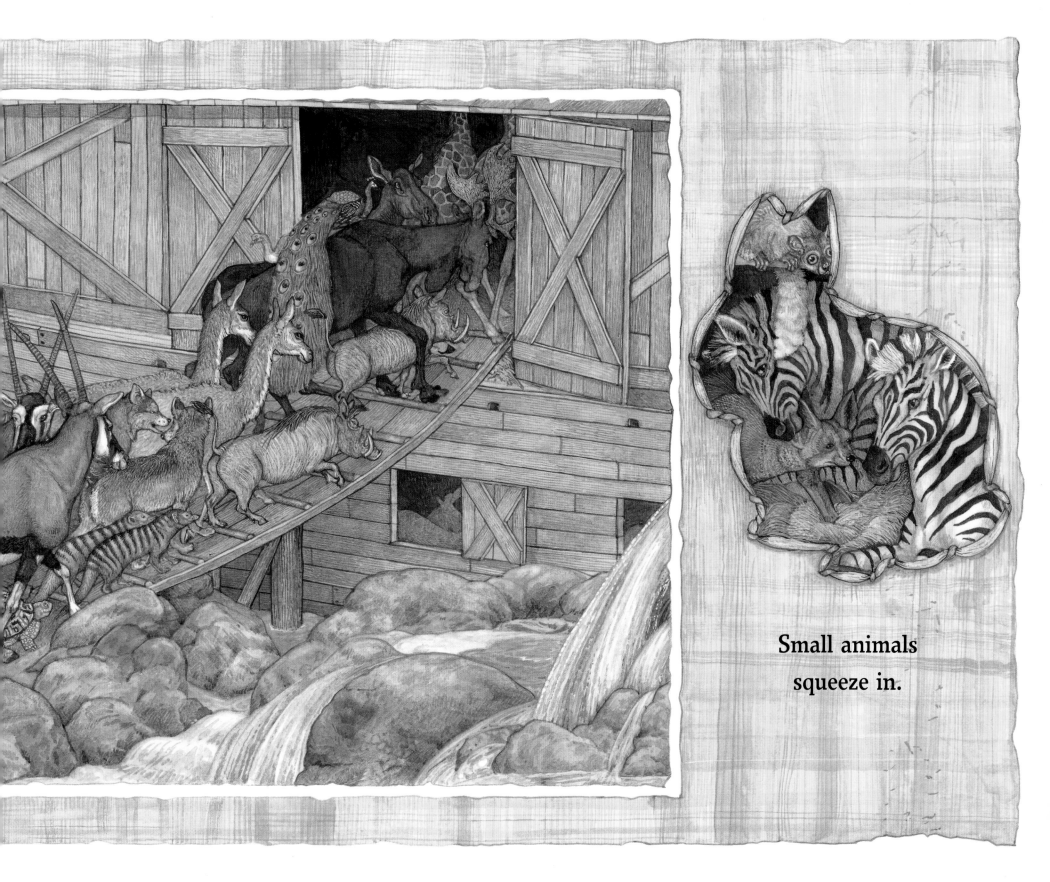

Small animals
squeeze in.

Flying creatures perch
on beams above.

Swimming animals
splish-splash below.

It rains and it rains.

Only the tops of mountains
poke up above the water.

It is crowded
inside the ark.

The animals push
and shove each other.

The ark rocks back and forth
like a giant cradle.

The animals fall asleep
all jumbled in together.

Everyone is asleep
except for me.

I tiptoe around
and untangle them.

It rains and rains
and rains

for forty days and
forty nights.

One morning I wake up.
I don't hear the rain.

I look out.
The sun is shining.

I run and wake up
Grandpa Noah.
He sends my dove off
to look for land.

She returns with
a fresh green leaf
from a new tree.

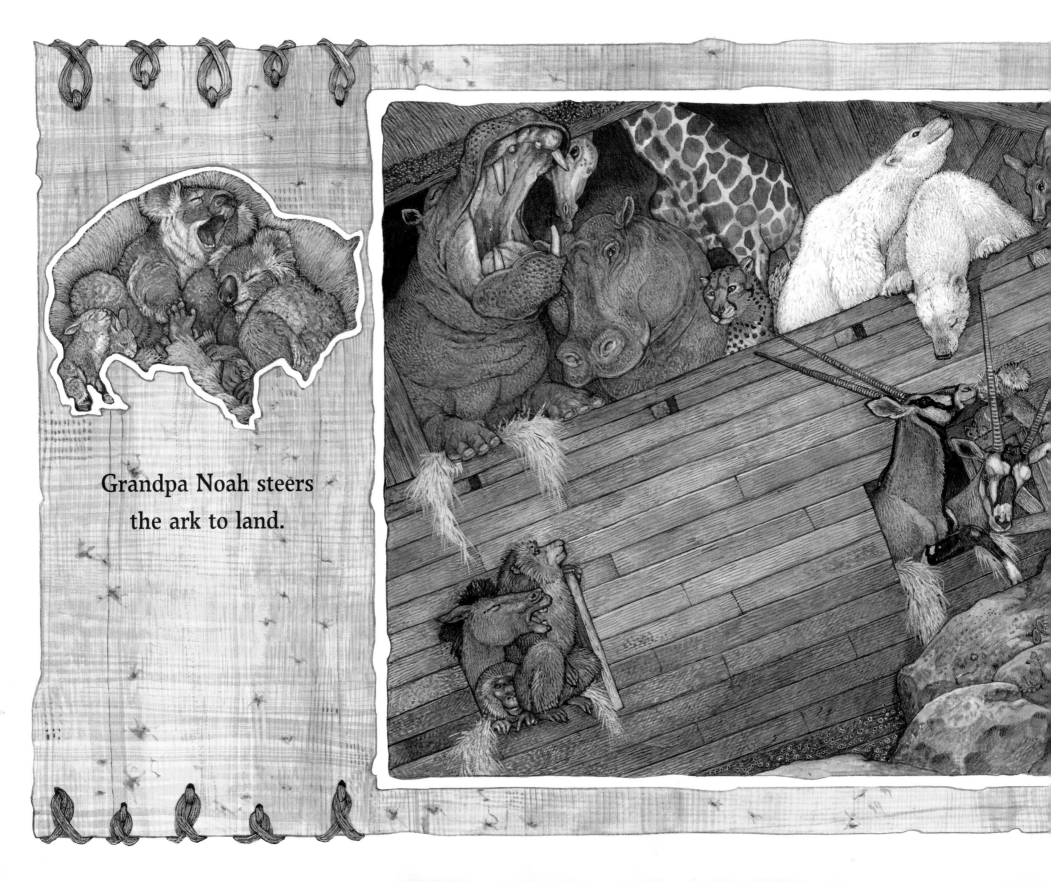

Grandpa Noah steers
the ark to land.

The animals wake up
and look out.

Two by two the animals
look for new homes.

East, west, north,
and south they go.

Some of the animals
stay with us.

Grandpa plants
a tiny seed.

Soon we will all be settled
into this new place.